QUEEN OF THE BLACK COAST

QUEEN OF THE BLACK COAST

Robert E. Howard

Queen of the Black Coast
Published by Classy Publishing @ 2021

www.classypublishing.com

ISBN: 978-93-5522-098-1

This is a work of fiction. Names, characters, businesses, places, events, locales, and incidents are either the products of the author's imagination or used in a fictitious manner. Any resemblance to actual persons, living or dead, or actual events is purely coincidental.

Cover design & Layout by satyacoverdesign.com
contact@satyacoverdesign.com

Contents

1

Conan Joins the Pirates

Believe green buds awaken in the spring,
That autumn paints the leaves with somber fire;
Believe I held my heart inviolate
To lavish on one man my hot desire.

THE SONG OF BÊLIT

Hoofs drummed down the street that sloped to the wharfs. The folk that yelled and scattered had only a fleeting glimpse of a mailed figure on a black stallion, a wide scarlet cloak flowing out on the wind. Far up the street came the shout and clatter of pursuit, but the horseman did not look back. He swept out onto the wharfs and jerked the plunging stallion back on its haunches at the very lip of the pier. Seamen gaped up at him, as they stood to the sweep and striped sail of a high-prowed, broad-waisted galley. The master, sturdy and black-bearded, stood in the bows, easing her away from the piles with a boat-hook. He yelled angrily as the horseman sprang from the saddle and with a long leap landed squarely on the mid-deck.

'Who invited you aboard?'

'Get under way!' roared the intruder with a fierce gesture that spattered red drops from his broadsword.

'But we're bound for the coasts of Kush!' expostulated the master.

'Then I'm for Kush! Push off, I tell you!' The other cast a quick glance up the street, along which a squad of horsemen were galloping; far behind them toiled a group of archers, crossbows on their shoulders.

'Can you pay for your passage?' demanded the master.

'I pay my way with steel!' roared the man in armor, brandishing the great sword that glittered bluely in the sun. 'By Crom, man, if you don't get under way, I'll drench this galley in the blood of its crew!'

The shipmaster was a good judge of men. One glance at the dark scarred face of the swordsman, hardened with passion, and he shouted a quick order, thrusting strongly against the piles. The galley wallowed out into clear water, the oars began to clack rhythmically; then a puff of wind filled the shimmering sail, the light ship heeled to the gust, then took her course like a swan, gathering headway as she skimmed along.

On the wharfs the riders were shaking their swords and shouting threats and commands that the ship put about, and yelling for the bowmen to hasten before the craft was out of arbalest range.

'Let them rave,' grinned the swordsman hardily. 'Do you keep her on her course, master steersman.'

The master descended from the small deck between the bows, made his way between the rows of oarsmen, and mounted the mid-deck. The stranger stood there with his back to the mast, eyes narrowed alertly, sword ready. The shipman eyed him steadily, careful not to make any move toward the long knife in his belt. He saw a tall powerfully built figure in a black scale-mail hauberk, burnished greaves and a blue-steel helmet from which jutted bull's horns highly polished. From the mailed shoulders fell the scarlet cloak, blowing in the sea-wind. A broad shagreen belt with a golden buckle held the scabbard of the broadsword he bore. Under the horned helmet a square-cut black mane contrasted with smoldering blue eyes.

'If we must travel together,' said the master, 'we may as well be at peace with each other. My name is Tito, licensed master-shipman of the ports of Argos. I am bound for Kush, to trade beads and silks and sugar and brass-hilted swords to the black kings for ivory, copra, copper ore, slaves and pearls.'

The swordsman glanced back at the rapidly receding docks, where the figures still gesticulated helplessly, evidently having trouble in finding a boat swift enough to overhaul the fast-sailing galley.

'I am Conan, a Cimmerian,' he answered. 'I came into Argos seeking employment, but with no wars forward, there was nothing to which I might turn my hand.'

'Why do the guardsmen pursue you?' asked Tito. 'Not that it's any of my business, but I thought perhaps——'

'I've nothing to conceal,' replied the Cimmerian. 'By Crom, though I've spent considerable time among you civilized peoples, your ways are still beyond my comprehension.

'Well, last night in a tavern, a captain in the king's guard offered violence to the sweetheart of a young soldier, who naturally ran him through. But it seems there is some cursed law against killing guardsmen, and the boy and his girl fled away. It was bruited about that I was seen with them, and so today I was haled into court, and a judge asked me where the lad had gone. I replied that since he was a friend of mine, I could not betray him. Then the court waxed wrath, and the judge talked a great deal about my duty to the state, and society, and other things I did not understand, and bade me tell where my friend had flown. By this time I was becoming wrathful myself, for I had explained my position.

'But I choked my ire and held my peace, and the judge squalled that I had shown contempt for the court, and that I should be hurled into a dungeon to rot until I betrayed my friend. So then, seeing they were all mad, I drew my sword and cleft the judge's skull; then I cut my way out of the court, and seeing the high constable's stallion tied near by, I rode for the wharfs, where I thought to find a ship bound for foreign parts.'

'Well,' said Tito hardily, 'the courts have fleeced me too often in suits with rich merchants for me to owe them any love. I'll have questions to answer if I ever anchor in that port again, but I can prove I acted under compulsion. You may as well put up your sword. We're peaceable sailors, and have nothing against you. Besides, it's as well to have a fighting-man like yourself on board. Come up to the poop-deck and we'll have a tankard of ale.'

'Good enough,' readily responded the Cimmerian, sheathing his sword.

The *Argus* was a small sturdy ship, typical of those trading-craft which ply between the ports of Zingara and Argos and the southern coasts, hugging the shoreline and seldom venturing far into the open ocean. It was high of stern, with a tall curving prow;

broad in the waist, sloping beautifully to stem and stern. It was guided by the long sweep from the poop, and propulsion was furnished mainly by the broad striped silk sail, aided by a jibsail. The oars were for use in tacking out of creeks and bays, and during calms. There were ten to the side, five fore and five aft of the small mid-deck. The most precious part of the cargo was lashed under this deck, and under the foredeck. The men slept on deck or between the rowers' benches, protected in bad weather by canopies. With twenty men at the oars, three at the sweep, and the shipmaster, the crew was complete.

So the *Argus* pushed steadily southward, with consistently fair weather. The sun beat down from day to day with fiercer heat, and the canopies were run up—striped silken cloths that matched the shimmering sail and the shining goldwork on the prow and along the gunwales.

They sighted the coast of Shem—long rolling meadowlands with the white crowns of the towers of cities in the distance, and horsemen with blue-black beards and hooked noses, who sat their steeds along the shore and eyed the galley with suspicion. She did not put in; there was scant profit in trade with the sons of Shem.

Nor did master Tito pull into the broad bay where the Styx river emptied its gigantic flood into the ocean, and the massive black castles of Khemi loomed over the blue waters. Ships did not put unasked into this port, where dusky sorcerers wove awful spells in the murk of sacrificial smoke mounting eternally from blood-stained altars where naked women screamed, and where Set, the Old Serpent, arch-demon of the Hyborians but god of the Stygians, was said to writhe his shining coils among his worshippers.

Master Tito gave that dreamy glass-floored bay a wide berth, even when a serpent-prowed gondola shot from behind a castellated point of land, and naked dusky women, with great red blossoms in their hair, stood and called to his sailors, and posed and postured brazenly.

Now no more shining towers rose inland. They had passed the southern borders of Stygia and were cruising along the coasts of Kush. The sea and the ways of the sea were never-ending mysteries to Conan, whose homeland was among the high hills of the northern uplands. The wanderer was no less of interest to the sturdy seamen, few of whom had ever seen one of his race.

They were characteristic Argosean sailors, short and stockily built. Conan towered above them, and no two of them could match his strength. They were hardy and robust, but his was the endurance and vitality of a wolf, his thews steeled and his nerves whetted by the hardness of his life in the world's wastelands. He was quick to laugh, quick and terrible in his wrath. He was a valiant trencherman, and strong drink was a passion and a weakness with him. Naïve as a child in many ways, unfamiliar with the sophistry of civilization, he was naturally intelligent, jealous of his rights, and dangerous as a hungry tiger. Young in years, he was hardened in warfare and wandering, and his sojourns in many lands were evident in his apparel. His horned helmet was such as was worn by the golden-haired Æsir of Nordheim; his hauberk and greaves were of the finest workmanship of Koth; the fine ring-mail which sheathed his arms and legs was of Nemedia; the blade at his girdle was a great Aquilonian broadsword; and his gorgeous scarlet cloak could have been spun nowhere but in Ophir.

So they beat southward, and master Tito began to look for the high-walled villages of the black people. But they found only smoking ruins on the shore of a bay, littered with naked black bodies. Tito swore.

'I had good trade here, aforetime. This is the work of pirates.'

'And if we meet them?' Conan loosened his great blade in its scabbard.

'Mine is no warship. We run, not fight. Yet if it came to a pinch, we have beaten off reavers before, and might do it again; unless it were Bêlit's *Tigress*.'

'Who is Bêlit?'

'The wildest she-devil unhanged. Unless I read the signs a-wrong, it was her butchers who destroyed that village on the bay. May I some day see her dangling from the yard-arm! She is called the queen of the black coast. She is a Shemite woman, who leads black raiders. They harry the shipping and have sent many a good tradesman to the bottom.'

From under the poop-deck Tito brought out quilted jerkins, steel caps, bows and arrows.

'Little use to resist if we're run down,' he grunted. 'But it rasps the soul to give up life without a struggle.'

* * *

It was just at sunrise when the lookout shouted a warning. Around the long point of an island off the starboard bow glided a long lethal shape, a slender serpentine galley, with a raised deck that ran from stem to stern. Forty oars on each side drove her swiftly through the water, and the low rail swarmed with naked blacks that chanted and clashed spears on oval shields. From the masthead floated a long crimson pennon.

'Bêlit!' yelled Tito, paling. 'Yare! Put her about! Into that creek-mouth! If we can beach her before they run us down, we have a chance to escape with our lives!'

So, veering sharply, the *Argus* ran for the line of surf that boomed along the palm-fringed shore, Tito striding back and forth, exhorting the panting rowers to greater efforts. The master's black beard bristled, his eyes glared.

'Give me a bow,' requested Conan. 'It's not my idea of a manly weapon, but I learned archery among the Hyrkanians, and it will go hard if I can't feather a man or so on yonder deck.'

Standing on the poop, he watched the serpent-like ship skimming lightly over the waters, and landsman though he was, it was evident to him that the *Argus* would never win that race. Already arrows, arching from the pirate's deck, were falling with a hiss into the sea, not twenty paces astern.

'We'd best stand to it,' growled the Cimmerian; 'else we'll all die with shafts in our backs, and not a blow dealt.'

'Bend to it, dogs!' roared Tito with a passionate gesture of his brawny fist. The bearded rowers grunted, heaved at the oars, while their muscles coiled and knotted, and sweat started out on their hides. The timbers of the stout little galley creaked and groaned as the men fairly ripped her through the water. The wind had fallen; the sail hung limp. Nearer crept the inexorable raiders, and they were still a good mile from the surf when one of the steersmen fell gagging across a sweep, a long arrow through his neck. Tito sprang to take his place, and Conan, bracing his feet wide on the heaving poop-deck, lifted his bow. He could see the details of the pirate plainly now. The rowers were protected by a line of raised mantelets along the sides, but the warriors dancing on the narrow deck were in full view. These were painted and plumed, and mostly naked, brandishing spears and spotted shields.

On the raised platform in the bows stood a slim figure whose white skin glistened in dazzling contrast to the glossy ebon hides about it. Bêlit, without a doubt. Conan drew the shaft to his ear—then some whim or qualm stayed his hand and sent the arrow through the body of a tall plumed spearman beside her.

Hand over hand the pirate galley was overhauling the lighter ship. Arrows fell in a rain about the *Argus*, and men cried out. All the steersmen were down, pincushioned, and Tito was handling the massive sweep alone, gasping black curses, his braced legs knots of straining thews. Then with a sob he sank down, a long shaft quivering in his sturdy heart. The *Argus* lost headway and rolled in the swell. The men shouted in confusion, and Conan took command in characteristic fashion.

'Up, lads!' he roared, loosing with a vicious twang of cord. 'Grab your steel and give these dogs a few knocks before they cut our throats! Useless to bend your backs any more: they'll board us ere we can row another fifty paces!'

In desperation the sailors abandoned their oars and snatched up their weapons. It was valiant, but useless. They had time for one flight of arrows before the pirate was upon them. With no one at the sweep, the *Argus* rolled broadside, and the steel-baked prow of the raider crashed into her amidships. Grappling-irons crunched into the side. From the lofty gunwales, the black pirates drove down a volley of shafts that tore through the quilted jackets of the doomed sailormen, then sprang down spear in hand to complete the slaughter. On the deck of the pirate lay half a dozen bodies, an earnest of Conan's archery.

The fight on the *Argus* was short and bloody. The stocky sailors, no match for the tall barbarians, were cut down to a man. Elsewhere the battle had taken a peculiar turn. Conan, on the high-pitched poop, was on a level with the pirate's deck. As the steel prow slashed into the *Argus*, he braced himself and kept his feet under the shock, casting away his bow. A tall corsair, bounding over the rail, was met in midair by the Cimmerian's great sword, which sheared him cleanly through the torso, so that his body fell one way and his legs another. Then, with a burst of fury that left a heap of mangled corpses along the gunwales, Conan was over the rail and on the deck of the *Tigress*.

In an instant he was the center of a hurricane of stabbing spears and lashing clubs. But he moved in a blinding blur of steel. Spears bent on his armor or swished empty air, and his sword sang its death-song. The fighting-madness of his race was upon him, and with a red mist of unreasoning fury wavering before his blazing eyes, he cleft skulls, smashed breasts, severed limbs, ripped out entrails, and littered the deck like a shambles with a ghastly harvest of brains and blood.

Invulnerable in his armor, his back against the mast, he heaped mangled corpses at his feet until his enemies gave back panting in rage and fear. Then as they lifted their spears to cast them, and he tensed himself to leap and die in the midst of them, a shrill cry froze the lifted arms. They stood like statues, the black giants poised for the spear-casts, the mailed swordsman with his dripping blade.

* * *

Bêlit sprang before the blacks, beating down their spears. She turned toward Conan, her bosom heaving, her eyes flashing. Fierce fingers of wonder caught at his heart. She was slender, yet formed like a goddess: at once lithe and voluptuous. Her only garment was a broad silken girdle. Her white ivory limbs and the ivory globes of her breasts drove a beat of fierce passion through the Cimmerian's pulse, even in the panting fury of battle. Her rich black hair, black as a Stygian night, fell in rippling burnished clusters down her supple back. Her dark eyes burned on the Cimmerian.

She was untamed as a desert wind, supple and dangerous as a she-panther. She came close to him, heedless of his great blade, dripping with blood of her warriors. Her supple thigh brushed against it, so close she came to the tall warrior. Her red lips parted as she stared up into his somber menacing eyes.

'Who are you?' she demanded. 'By Ishtar, I have never seen your like, though I have ranged the sea from the coasts of Zingara to the fires of the ultimate south. Whence come you?'

'From Argos,' he answered shortly, alert for treachery. Let her slim hand move toward the jeweled dagger in her girdle, and a buffet of his open hand would stretch her senseless on the deck. Yet in his heart he did not fear; he had held too many women, civilized or barbaric, in his iron-thewed arms, not to recognize the light that burned in the eyes of this one.

'You are no soft Hyborian!' she exclaimed. 'You are fierce and hard as a gray wolf. Those eyes were never dimmed by city lights; those thews were never softened by life amid marble walls.'

'I am Conan, a Cimmerian,' he answered.

To the people of the exotic climes, the north was a mazy half-mythical realm, peopled with ferocious blue-eyed giants who occasionally descended from their icy fastnesses with torch and sword. Their raids had never taken them as far south as Shem, and this daughter of Shem made no distinction between Æsir, Vanir or Cimmerian. With the unerring instinct of the elemental feminine, she knew she had found her lover, and his race meant naught, save as it invested him with the glamor of far lands.

'And I am Bêlit,' she cried, as one might say, 'I am queen.'

'Look at me, Conan!' She threw wide her arms. 'I am Bêlit, queen of the black coast. Oh, tiger of the North, you are cold as the snowy mountains which bred you. Take me and crush me with your fierce love! Go with me to the ends of the earth and the ends of the sea! I am a queen by fire and steel and slaughter—be thou my king!'

His eyes swept the blood-stained ranks, seeking expressions of wrath or jealousy. He saw none. The fury was gone from the ebon faces. He realized that to these men Bêlit was more than a woman: a goddess whose will was unquestioned. He glanced at the *Argus*, wallowing in the crimson sea-wash, heeling far over, her decks awash, held up by the grappling-irons. He glanced at the blue-fringed shore, at the far green hazes of the ocean, at the vibrant figure which stood before him; and his barbaric soul stirred within him. To quest these shining blue realms with that white-skinned young tiger-cat—to love, laugh, wander and pillage—

'I'll sail with you,' he grunted, shaking the red drops from his blade.

'Ho, N'Yaga!' her voice twanged like a bowstring. 'Fetch herbs and dress your master's wounds! The rest of you bring aboard the plunder and cast off.'

As Conan sat with his back against the poop-rail, while the old shaman attended to the cuts on his hands and limbs, the cargo of the ill-fated *Argus* was quickly shifted aboard the *Tigress* and stored in small cabins below deck. Bodies of the crew and of fallen pirates were cast overboard to the swarming sharks, while wounded blacks were laid in the waist to be bandaged. Then the grappling-irons were cast off, and as the *Argus* sank silently into the blood-flecked waters, the *Tigress* moved off southward to the rhythmic clack of the oars.

As they moved out over the glassy blue deep, Bêlit came to the poop. Her eyes were burning like those of a she-panther in the dark as she tore off her ornaments, her sandals and her silken girdle and cast them at his feet. Rising on tiptoe, arms stretched upward, a quivering line of naked white, she cried to the desperate horde: 'Wolves of the blue sea, behold ye now the dance—the mating-dance of Bêlit, whose fathers were kings of Askalon!'

And she danced, like the spin of a desert whirlwind, like the leaping of a quenchless flame, like the urge of creation and the urge of death. Her white feet spurned the blood-stained deck and dying men forgot death as they gazed frozen at her. Then, as the white stars glimmered through the blue velvet dusk, making her whirling body a blur of ivory fire, with a wild cry she threw herself at Conan's feet, and the blind flood of the Cimmerian's desire swept all else away as he crushed her panting form against the black plates of his corseleted breast.

2

The Black Lotus

In that dead citadel of crumbling stone
Her eyes were snared by that unholy sheen,
And curious madness took me by the throat,
As of a rival lover thrust between.
THE SONG OF BÊLIT

The *Tigress* ranged the sea, and the black villages shuddered. Tomtoms beat in the night, with a tale that the she-devil of the sea had found a mate, an iron man whose wrath was as that of a wounded lion. And survivors of butchered Stygian ships named Bêlit with curses, and a white warrior with fierce blue eyes; so the Stygian princes remembered this man long and long, and their memory was a bitter tree which bore crimson fruit in the years to come.

But heedless as a vagrant wind, the *Tigress* cruised the southern coasts, until she anchored at the mouth of a broad sullen river, whose banks were jungle-clouded walls of mystery.

'This is the river Zarkheba, which is Death,' said Bêlit. 'Its waters are poisonous. See how dark and murky they run? Only venomous reptiles live in that river. The black people shun it. Once a Stygian galley, fleeing from me, fled up the river and vanished. I anchored in this very spot, and days later, the galley came floating down the dark waters, its decks blood-stained and deserted. Only one man was on board, and he was mad and died gibbering. The cargo was intact, but the crew had vanished into silence and mystery.

'My lover, I believe there is a city somewhere on that river. I have heard tales of giant towers and walls glimpsed afar off by sailors who dared go part-way up the river. We fear nothing: Conan, let us go and sack that city!'

Conan agreed. He generally agreed to her plans. Hers was the mind that directed their raids, his the arm that carried out her ideas. It mattered little to him where they sailed or whom they fought, so long as they sailed and fought. He found the life good.

Battle and raid had thinned their crew; only some eighty spearmen remained, scarcely enough to work the long galley. But Bêlit would not take the time to make the long cruise southward to the island kingdoms where she recruited her buccaneers. She was afire with eagerness for her latest venture; so the *Tigress* swung into the river mouth, the oarsmen pulling strongly as she breasted the broad current.

They rounded the mysterious bend that shut out the sight of the sea, and sunset found them forging steadily against the sluggish flow, avoiding sandbars where strange reptiles coiled. Not even a crocodile did they see, nor any four-legged beast or winged bird coming down to the water's edge to drink. On through the blackness that preceded moonrise they drove, between banks that were solid palisades of darkness, whence came mysterious rustlings and stealthy footfalls, and the gleam of grim eyes. And once an inhuman voice was lifted in awful mockery—the cry of an ape, Bêlit said, adding that the souls of evil men were imprisoned in these man-like animals as punishment for past crimes. But Conan doubted, for once, in a gold-barred cage in an Hyrkanian city, he had seen an abysmal sad-eyed beast which men told him was an ape, and there had been about it naught of the demoniac malevolence which vibrated in the shrieking laughter that echoed from the black jungle.

Then the moon rose, a splash of blood, ebony-barred, and the jungle awoke in horrific bedlam to greet it. Roars and howls and yells set the black warriors to trembling, but all this noise, Conan noted, came from farther back in the jungle, as if the beasts no less than men shunned the black waters of Zarkheba.

Rising above the black denseness of the trees and above the waving fronds, the moon silvered the river, and their wake became a rippling scintillation of phosphorescent bubbles that widened like a shining road of bursting jewels. The oars dipped into the shining water and came up sheathed in frosty silver. The plumes on the warrior's headpiece nodded in the wind, and the gems on sword-hilts and harness sparkled frostily.

The cold light struck icy fire from the jewels in Bêlit's clustered black locks as she stretched her lithe figure on a leopardskin thrown on the deck. Supported on her elbows, her chin resting on her slim hands, she gazed up into the face of Conan, who lounged beside her, his black mane stirring in the faint breeze. Bêlit's eyes were dark jewels burning in the moonlight.

'Mystery and terror are about us, Conan, and we glide into the realm of horror and death,' she said. 'Are you afraid?'

A shrug of his mailed shoulders was his only answer.

'I am not afraid either,' she said meditatively. 'I was never afraid. I have looked into the naked fangs of Death too often. Conan, do you fear the gods?'

'I would not tread on their shadow,' answered the barbarian conservatively. 'Some gods are strong to harm, others, to aid; at least so say their priests. Mitra of the Hyborians must be a strong god, because his people have builded their cities over the world. But even the Hyborians fear Set. And Bel, god of thieves, is a good god. When I was a thief in Zamora I learned of him.'

'What of your own gods? I have never heard you call on them.'

'Their chief is Crom. He dwells on a great mountain. What use to call on him? Little he cares if men live or die. Better to be silent than to call his attention to you; he will send you dooms, not fortune! He is grim and loveless, but at birth he breathes power to strive and slay into a man's soul. What else shall men ask of the gods?'

'But what of the worlds beyond the river of death?' she persisted.

'There is no hope here or hereafter in the cult of my people,' answered Conan. 'In this world men struggle and suffer vainly, finding pleasure only in the bright madness of battle; dying, their souls enter a gray misty realm of clouds and icy winds, to wander cheerlessly throughout eternity.'

Bêlit shuddered. 'Life, bad as it is, is better than such a destiny. What do you believe, Conan?'

He shrugged his shoulders. 'I have known many gods. He who denies them is as blind as he who trusts them too deeply. I seek not beyond death. It may be the blackness averred by the Nemedian skeptics, or Crom's realm of ice and cloud, or the snowy plains and vaulted halls of the Nordheimer's Valhalla. I know not, nor do I care. Let me live deep while I live; let me know the rich juices of red meat and stinging wine on my palate, the hot embrace of white arms, the mad exultation of battle when the blue blades flame and crimson, and I am content. Let teachers and priests and philosophers brood over questions of reality and illusion. I know this: if life is illusion, then I am no less an illusion, and being thus, the illusion is real to me. I live, I burn with life, I love, I slay, and am content.'

'But the gods are real,' she said, pursuing her own line of thought. 'And above all are the gods of the Shemites—Ishtar and Ashtoreth and Derketo and Adonis. Bel, too, is Shemitish, for he was born in ancient Shumir, long, long ago and went forth laughing, with curled beard and impish wise eyes, to steal the gems of the kings of old times.

'There is life beyond death, I know, and I know this, too, Conan of Cimmeria—' she rose lithely to her knees and caught him in a pantherish embrace—'my love is stronger than any death! I have lain in your arms, panting with the violence of our love;

you have held and crushed and conquered me, drawing my soul to your lips with the fierceness of your bruising kisses. My heart is welded to your heart, my soul is part of your soul! Were I still in death and you fighting for life, I would come back from the abyss to aid you—aye, whether my spirit floated with the purple sails on the crystal sea of paradise, or writhed in the molten flames of hell! I am yours, and all the gods and all their eternities shall not sever us!'

* * *

A scream rang from the lookout in the bows. Thrusting Bêlit aside, Conan bounded up, his sword a long silver glitter in the moonlight, his hair bristling at what he saw. The black warrior dangled above the deck, supported by what seemed a dark pliant tree trunk arching over the rail. Then he realized that it was a gigantic serpent which had writhed its glistening length up the side of the bow and gripped the luckless warrior in its jaws. Its dripping scales shone leprously in the moonlight as it reared its form high above the deck, while the stricken man screamed and writhed like a mouse in the fangs of a python. Conan rushed into the bows, and swinging his great sword, hewed nearly through the giant trunk, which was thicker than a man's body. Blood drenched the rails as the dying monster swayed far out, still gripping its victim, and sank into the river, coil by coil, lashing the water to bloody foam, in which man and reptile vanished together.

Thereafter Conan kept the lookout watch himself, but no other horror came crawling up from the murky depths, and as dawn whitened over the jungle, he sighted the black fangs of towers jutting up among the trees. He called Bêlit, who slept on the deck, wrapped in his scarlet cloak; and she sprang to his side, eyes blazing. Her lips were parted to call orders to her warriors to take up bow and spears; then her lovely eyes widened.

It was but the ghost of a city on which they looked when they cleared a jutting jungle-clad point and swung in toward the in-curving shore. Weeds and rank river grass grew between the stones of broken piers and shattered paves that had once been streets and spacious plazas and broad courts. From all sides except that toward the river, the jungle crept in, masking fallen columns and crumbling mounds with poisonous green. Here and there buckling towers reeled drunkenly against the morning sky, and broken pillars jutted up among the decaying walls. In the center space a marble pyramid was spired by a slim column, and on its pinnacle sat or squatted something that Conan supposed to be an image until his keen eyes detected life in it.

'It is a great bird,' said one of the warriors, standing in the bows.

'It is a monster bat,' insisted another.

'It is an ape,' said Bêlit.

Just then the creature spread broad wings and flapped off into the jungle.

'A winged ape,' said old N'Yaga uneasily. 'Better we had cut our throats than come to this place. It is haunted.'

Bêlit mocked at his superstitions and ordered the galley run inshore and tied to the crumbling wharfs. She was the first to spring ashore, closely followed by Conan, and after them trooped the ebon-skinned pirates, white plumes waving in the morning wind, spears ready, eyes rolling dubiously at the surrounding jungle.

Over all brooded a silence as sinister as that of a sleeping serpent. Bêlit posed picturesquely among the ruins, the vibrant life in her lithe figure contrasting strangely with the desolation and decay about her. The sun flamed up slowly, sullenly, above the jungle, flooding the towers with a dull gold that left shadows lurking beneath the tottering walls. Bêlit pointed to a slim round tower that reeled on its rotting base. A broad expanse of cracked, grass-grown slabs led up to it, flanked by fallen columns, and before it stood a massive altar. Bêlit went swiftly along the ancient floor and stood before it.

'This was the temple of the old ones,' she said. 'Look—you can see the channels for the blood along the sides of the altar, and the rains of ten thousand years have not washed the dark stains from them. The walls have all fallen away, but this stone block defies time and the elements.'

'But who were these old ones?' demanded Conan.

She spread her slim hands helplessly. 'Not even in legendary is this city mentioned. But look at the handholes at either end of the altar! Priests often conceal their treasures beneath their altars. Four of you lay hold and see if you can lift it.'

She stepped back to make room for them, glancing up at the tower which loomed drunkenly above them. Three of the strongest blacks had gripped the handholes cut into the stone—curiously unsuited to human hands—when Bêlit sprang back with a sharp cry. They froze in their places, and Conan, bending to aid them, wheeled with a startled curse.

'A snake in the grass,' she said, backing away. 'Come and slay it; the rest of you bend your backs to the stone.'

Conan came quickly toward her, another taking his place. As he impatiently scanned the grass for the reptile, the giant blacks braced their feet, grunted and heaved with their huge muscles coiling and straining under their ebon skin. The altar did not come off the ground, but it revolved suddenly on its side. And simultaneously there was a grinding rumble above and the tower came crashing down, covering the four black men with broken masonry.

A cry of horror rose from their comrades. Bêlit's slim fingers dug into Conan's arm-muscles. 'There was no serpent,' she whispered. 'It was but a ruse to call you away. I feared; the old ones guarded their treasure well. Let us clear away the stones.'

With herculean labor they did so, and lifted out the mangled bodies of the four men. And under them, stained with their blood, the pirates found a crypt carved in the solid stone. The altar, hinged curiously with stone rods and sockets on one side, had served as its lid. And at first glance the crypt seemed brimming with liquid fire, catching the early light with a million blazing facets. Undreamable wealth lay before the eyes of the gaping pirates; diamonds, rubies, bloodstones, sapphires, turquoises, moonstones, opals, emeralds, amethysts, unknown gems that shone like the eyes of evil women. The crypt was filled to the brim with bright stones that the morning sun struck into lambent flame.

With a cry Bêlit dropped to her knees among the blood-stained rubble on the brink and thrust her white arms shoulder-deep into that pool of splendor. She withdrew them, clutching something that brought another cry to her lips—a long string of crimson stones that were like clots of frozen blood strung on a thick gold wire. In their glow the golden sunlight changed to bloody haze.

Bêlit's eyes were like a woman's in a trance. The Shemite soul finds a bright drunkenness in riches and material splendor, and the sight of this treasure might have shaken the soul of a sated emperor of Shushan.

'Take up the jewels, dogs!' her voice was shrill with her emotions.

'Look!' a muscular black arm stabbed toward the *Tigress*, and Bêlit wheeled, her crimson lips a-snarl, as if she expected to see a rival corsair sweeping in to despoil her of her plunder. But from the gunwales of the ship a dark shape rose, soaring away over the jungle.

'The devil-ape has been investigating the ship,' muttered the blacks uneasily.

'What matter?' cried Bêlit with a curse, raking back a rebellious lock with an impatient hand. 'Make a litter of spears ând mantles to bear these jewels— where the devil are you going?'

'To look to the galley,' grunted Conan. 'That bat-thing might have knocked a hole in the bottom, for all we know.'

He ran swiftly down the cracked wharf and sprang aboard. A moment's swift examination below decks, and he swore heartily, casting a clouded glance in the direction the bat-being had vanished. He returned hastily to Bêlit, superintending the plundering of the crypt. She had looped the necklace about her neck, and on her naked white bosom the red clots glimmered darkly. A huge naked black stood crotch-deep in the jewel-brimming crypt, scooping up great handfuls of splendor to pass them to eager hands above. Strings of frozen iridescence hung between his dusky fingers; drops of red fire dripped from his hands, piled high with starlight and rainbow. It was as if a black titan stood straddle-legged in the bright pits of hell, his lifted hands full of stars.

'That flying devil has staved in the water-casks,' said Conan. 'If we hadn't been so dazed by these stones we'd have heard the noise. We were fools not to have left a man on guard. We can't drink this river water. I'll take twenty men and search for fresh water in the jungle.'

She looked at him vaguely, in her eyes the blank blaze of her strange passion, her fingers working at the gems on her breast.

'Very well,' she said absently, hardly heeding him. 'I'll get the loot aboard.'

* * *

The jungle closed quickly about them, changing the light from gold to gray. From the arching green branches creepers dangled like pythons. The warriors fell into single file, creeping through the primordial twilights like black phantoms following a white ghost.

Underbrush was not so thick as Conan had anticipated. The ground was spongy but not slushy. Away from the river, it sloped gradually upward. Deeper and deeper they plunged into the green waving depths, and still there was no sign of water, either running stream or stagnant pool. Conan halted suddenly, his warriors freezing into basaltic statues. In the tense silence that followed, the Cimmerian shook his head irritably.

'Go ahead,' he grunted to a sub-chief, N'Gora. 'March straight on until you can no longer see me; then stop and wait for me. I believe we're being followed. I heard something.'

The blacks shuffled their feet uneasily, but did as they were told. As they swung onward, Conan stepped quickly behind a great tree, glaring back along the way they had come. From that leafy fastness anything might emerge. Nothing occurred; the faint sounds of the marching spearmen faded in the distance. Conan suddenly realized that the air was impregnated with an alien and exotic scent. Something gently brushed his temple. He turned quickly. From a cluster of green, curiously leafed stalks, great black blossoms nodded at him. One of these had touched him. They seemed to beckon him, to arch their pliant stems toward him. They spread and rustled, though no wind blew.

He recoiled, recognizing the black lotus, whose juice was death, and whose scent brought dream-haunted slumber. But already he felt a subtle lethargy stealing over him. He sought to lift his sword, to hew down the serpentine stalks, but his arm hung lifeless at his side. He opened his mouth to shout to his warriors, but only a faint rattle issued. The next instant, with appalling suddenness, the jungle waved and dimmed out before his eyes; he did not hear the screams that burst out awfully not far away, as his knees collapsed, letting him pitch limply to the earth. Above his prostrate form the great black blossoms nodded in the windless air.

3

The Horror in the Jungle

Was it a dream the nighted lotus brought?
Then curst the dream that bought my sluggish life;
And curst each laggard hour that does not see
Hot blood drip blackly from the crimsoned knife.
THE SONG OF BÊLIT

First there was the blackness of an utter void, with the cold winds of cosmic space blowing through it. Then shapes, vague, monstrous and evanescent, rolled in dim panorama through the expanse of nothingness, as if the darkness were taking material form. The winds blew and a vortex formed, a whirling pyramid of roaring blackness. From it grew Shape and Dimension; then suddenly, like clouds dispersing, the darkness rolled away on either hand and a huge city of dark green stone rose on the bank of a wide river, flowing through an illimitable plain. Through this city moved beings of alien configuration.

Cast in the mold of humanity, they were distinctly not men. They were winged and of heroic proportions;

not a branch on the mysterious stalk of evolution that culminated in man, but the ripe blossom on an alien tree, separate and apart from that stalk. Aside from their wings, in physical appearance they resembled man only as man in his highest form resembles the great apes. In spiritual, esthetic and intellectual development they were superior to man as man is superior to the gorilla. But when they reared their colossal city, man's primal ancestors had not yet risen from the slime of the primordial seas.

These beings were mortal, as are all things built of flesh and blood. They lived, loved and died, though the individual span of life was enormous. Then, after uncounted millions of years, the Change began. The vista shimmered and wavered, like a picture thrown on a windblown curtain. Over the city and the land the ages flowed as waves flow over a beach, and each wave brought alterations. Somewhere on the planet the magnetic centers were shifting; the great glaciers and ice-fields were withdrawing toward the new poles.

The littoral of the great river altered. Plains turned into swamps that stank with reptilian life. Where fertile meadows had rolled, forests reared up, growing into dank jungles. The changing ages wrought on the inhabitants of the city as well. They did not migrate to fresher lands. Reasons inexplicable to humanity held them to the ancient city and their doom. And as that once rich and mighty land sank deeper and deeper into the black mire of the sunless jungle, so into the chaos of squalling jungle life sank the people of the city. Terrific convulsions shook the earth; the nights were lurid with spouting volcanoes that fringed the dark horizons with red pillars.

After an earthquake that shook down the outer walls and highest towers of the city, and caused the river to run black for days with some lethal substance spewed up from the subterranean depths, a frightful chemical change became apparent in the waters the folk had drunk for millenniums uncountable.

Many died who drank of it; and in those who lived, the drinking wrought change, subtle, gradual and grisly. In adapting themselves to the changing conditions, they had sunk far below their original level. But the lethal waters altered them even more horribly, from generation to more bestial generation. They who had been winged gods became pinioned demons, with all that remained of their ancestors' vast knowledge distorted and perverted and twisted into ghastly paths. As they had risen higher than mankind might dream, so they sank lower than man's maddest nightmares reach. They died fast, by cannibalism, and horrible feuds fought out in the murk of the midnight jungle. And at last among the lichen-grown ruins of their city only a single shape lurked, a stunted abhorrent perversion of nature.

Then for the first time humans appeared: dark-skinned, hawk-faced men in copper and leather harness, bearing bows—the warriors of pre-historic Stygia. There were only fifty of them, and they were haggard and gaunt with starvation and prolonged effort, stained and scratched with jungle-wandering, with blood-crusted bandages that told of fierce fighting. In their minds was a tale of warfare and defeat, and flight before a stronger tribe which drove them ever southward, until they lost themselves in the green ocean of jungle and river.

Exhausted they lay down among the ruins where red blossoms that bloom but once in a century waved in the full moon, and sleep fell upon them. And as they slept, a hideous shape crept red-eyed from the shadows and performed weird and awful rites about and above each sleeper. The moon hung in the shadowy sky, painting the jungle red and black; above the sleepers glimmered the crimson blossoms, like splashes of blood. Then the moon went down and the eyes of the necromancer were red jewels set in the ebony of night.

When dawn spread its white veil over the river, there were no men to be seen: only a hairy winged horror that squatted in the center of a ring of fifty great spotted hyenas that pointed quivering muzzles to the ghastly sky and howled like souls in hell.

Then scene followed scene so swiftly that each tripped over the heels of its predecessor. There was a confusion of movement, a writhing and melting of lights and shadows, against a background of black jungle, green stone ruins and murky river. Black men came up the river in long boats with skulls grinning on the prows, or stole stooping through the trees, spear in hand. They fled screaming through the dark from red eyes and slavering fangs. Howls of dying men shook the shadows; stealthy feet padded through the gloom, vampire eyes blazed redly. There were grisly feasts beneath the moon, across whose red disk a bat-like shadow incessantly swept.

Then abruptly, etched clearly in contrast to these impressionistic glimpses, around the jungled point in the whitening dawn swept a long galley, thronged with shining ebon figures, and in the bows stood a white-skinned ghost in blue steel.

It was at this point that Conan first realized that he was dreaming. Until that instant he had had no consciousness of individual existence. But as he saw himself treading the boards of the *Tigress*, he recognized both the existence and the dream, although he did not awaken.

Even as he wondered, the scene shifted abruptly to a jungle glade where N'Gora and nineteen black spearmen stood, as if awaiting someone. Even as he realized that it was he for whom they waited, a horror swooped down from the skies and their stolidity was broken by yells of fear. Like men maddened by terror, they threw away their weapons and raced wildly through the jungle, pressed close by the slavering monstrosity that flapped its wings above them.

* * *

Chaos and confusion followed this vision, during which Conan feebly struggled to awake. Dimly he seemed to see himself lying under a nodding cluster of black blossoms, while from the bushes a hideous shape crept toward him. With a savage effort he broke the unseen bonds which held him to his dreams, and started upright.

Bewilderment was in the glare he cast about him. Near him swayed the dusky lotus, and he hastened to draw away from it.

In the spongy soil near by there was a track as if an animal had put out a foot, preparatory to emerging from the bushes, then had withdrawn it. It looked like the spoor of an unbelievably large hyena.

He yelled for N'Gora. Primordial silence brooded over the jungle, in which his yells sounded brittle and hollow as mockery. He could not see the sun, but his wilderness-trained instinct told him the day was near its end. A panic rose in him at the thought that he had lain senseless for hours. He hastily followed the tracks of the spearmen, which lay plain in the damp loam before him. They ran in single file, and he soon emerged into a glade—to stop short, the skin crawling between his shoulders as he recognized it as the glade he had seen in his lotus-drugged dream. Shields and spears lay scattered about as if dropped in headlong flight.

And from the tracks which led out of the glade and deeper into the fastnesses, Conan knew that the spearmen had fled, wildly. The footprints overlay one another; they weaved blindly among the trees. And with startling suddenness the hastening Cimmerian came out of the jungle onto a hill-like rock which sloped steeply, to break off abruptly in a sheer precipice forty feet high. And something crouched on the brink.

At first Conan thought it to be a great black gorilla. Then he saw that it was a giant black man that crouched ape-like, long arms dangling, froth dripping from the loose lips. It was not until, with a sobbing cry, the creature lifted huge hands and rushed towards him, that Conan recognized N'Gora. The black man gave no heed to Conan's shout as he charged, eyes rolled up to display the whites, teeth gleaming, face an inhuman mask.

With his skin crawling with the horror that madness always instils in the sane, Conan passed his sword through the black man's body; then, avoiding the hooked hands that clawed at him as N'Gora sank down, he strode to the edge of the cliff.

For an instant he stood looking down into the jagged rocks below, where lay N'Gora's spearmen, in limp, distorted attitudes that told of crushed limbs and splintered bones. Not one moved. A cloud of huge black flies buzzed loudly above the blood-splashed stones; the ants had already begun to gnaw at the corpses. On the trees about sat birds of prey, and a jackal, looking up and seeing the man on the cliff, slunk furtively away.

For a little space Conan stood motionless. Then he wheeled and ran back the way he had come, flinging himself with reckless haste through the tall grass and bushes, hurdling creepers that sprawled snake-like across his path. His sword swung low in his right hand, and an unaccustomed pallor tinged his dark face.

The silence that reigned in the jungle was not broken. The sun had set and great shadows rushed upward from the slime of the black earth. Through the gigantic shades of lurking death and grim desolation Conan was a speeding glimmer of scarlet and blue steel. No sound in all the solitude was heard except his own quick panting as he burst from the shadows into the dim twilight of the river-shore.

He saw the galley shouldering the rotten wharf, the ruins reeling drunkenly in the gray half-light.

And here and there among the stones were spots of raw bright color, as if a careless hand had splashed with a crimson brush.

Again Conan looked on death and destruction. Before him lay his spearmen, nor did they rise to salute him. From the jungle-edge to the riverbank, among the rotting pillars and along the broken piers they lay, torn and mangled and half devoured, chewed travesties of men.

All about the bodies and pieces of bodies were swarms of huge footprints, like those of hyenas.

Conan came silently upon the pier, approaching the galley above whose deck was suspended something that glimmered ivory-white in the faint twilight. Speechless, the Cimmerian looked on the Queen of the Black Coast as she hung from the yard-arm of her own galley. Between the yard and her white throat stretched a line of crimson clots that shone like blood in the gray light.

4

The Attack from the Air

The shadows were black around him,
The dripping jaws gaped wide,
Thicker than rain the red drops fell;
But my love was fiercer than
Death's black spell,
Nor all the iron walls of hell
Could keep me from his side.

THE SONG OF BÊLIT

The jungle was a black colossus that locked the ruin-littered glade in ebon arms. The moon had not risen; the stars were flecks of hot amber in a breathless sky that reeked of death. On the pyramid among the fallen towers sat Conan the Cimmerian like an iron statue, chin propped on massive fists. Out in the black shadows stealthy feet padded and red eyes glimmered. The dead lay as they had fallen. But on the deck of the *Tigress*, on a pyre of broken benches, spear-shafts and leopardskins, lay the Queen of the Black Coast in her last sleep, wrapped in Conan's scarlet cloak. Like a true queen she lay, with her plunder heaped high about her: silks, cloth-of-gold, silver braid, casks of gems and golden coins, silver ingots, jeweled daggers and teocallis of gold wedges.

But of the plunder of the accursed city, only the sullen waters of Zarkheba could tell where Conan had thrown it with a heathen curse. Now he sat grimly on the pyramid, waiting for his unseen foes. The black fury in his soul drove out all fear. What shapes would emerge from the blackness he knew not, nor did he care.

He no longer doubted the visions of the black lotus. He understood that while waiting for him in the glade, N'Gora and his comrades had been terror-stricken by the winged monster swooping upon them from the sky, and fleeing in blind panic, had fallen over the cliff, all except their chief, who had somehow escaped their fate, though not madness. Meanwhile, or immediately after, or perhaps before, the destruction of those on the riverbank had been accomplished. Conan did not doubt that the slaughter along the river had been massacre rather than battle. Already unmanned by their superstitious fears, the blacks might well have died without striking a blow in their own defense when attacked by their inhuman foes.

Why he had been spared so long, he did not understand, unless the malign entity which ruled the river meant to keep him alive to torture him with grief and fear. All pointed to a human or superhuman intelligence—the breaking of the water-casks to divide the forces, the driving of the blacks over the cliff, and last and greatest, the grim jest of the crimson necklace knotted like a hangman's noose about Bêlit's white neck.

Having apparently saved the Cimmerian for the choicest victim, and extracted the last ounce of exquisite mental torture, it was likely that the unknown enemy would conclude the drama by sending him after the other victims. No smile bent Conan's grim lips at the thought, but his eyes were lit with iron laughter.

The moon rose, striking fire from the Cimmerian's horned helmet. No call awoke the echoes; yet suddenly the night grew tense and the jungle held its breath. Instinctively Conan loosened the great sword in its sheath. The pyramid on which he rested was four-sided, one—the side toward the jungle—carved in broad steps. In his hand was a Shemite bow, such as Bêlit had taught her pirates to use. A heap of arrows lay at his feet, feathered ends towards him, as he rested on one knee.

Something moved in the blackness under the trees. Etched abruptly in the rising moon, Conan saw a darkly blocked-out head and shoulders, brutish in outline. And now from the shadows dark shapes came silently, swiftly, running low—twenty great spotted hyenas. Their slavering fangs flashed in the moonlight, their eyes blazed as no true beast's eyes ever blazed.

Twenty: then the spears of the pirates had taken toll of the pack, after all. Even as he thought this, Conan drew nock to ear, and at the twang of the string a flame-eyed shadow bounded high and fell writhing. The rest did not falter; on they came, and like a rain of death among them fell the arrows of the Cimmerian, driven with all the force and accuracy of steely thews backed by a hate hot as the slag-heaps of hell.

In his berserk fury he did not miss; the air was filled with feathered destruction. The havoc wrought among the onrushing pack was breathtaking. Less than half of them reached the foot of the pyramid. Others dropped upon the broad steps. Glaring down into the blazing eyes, Conan knew these creatures were not beasts; it was not merely in their unnatural size that he sensed a blasphemous difference. They exuded an aura tangible as the black mist rising from a corpse-littered swamp. By what godless alchemy these beings had been brought into existence, he could not guess; but he knew he faced diabolism blacker than the Well of Skelos.

Springing to his feet, he bent his bow powerfully and drove his last shaft point blank at a great hairy shape that soared up at his throat. The arrow was a flying beam of moonlight that flashed onward with but a blur in its course, but the were-beast plunged convulsively in midair and crashed headlong, shot through and through.

Then the rest were on him, in a nightmare rush of blazing eyes and dripping fangs. His fiercely driven sword shore the first asunder; then the desperate impact of the others bore him down. He crushed a narrow skull with the pommel of his hilt, feeling the bone splinter and blood and brains gush over his hand; then, dropping the sword, useless at such deadly close quarters, he caught at the throats of the two horrors which were ripping and tearing at him in silent fury. A foul acrid scent almost stifled him, his own sweat blinded him. Only his mail saved him from being ripped to ribbons in an instant. The next, his naked right hand locked on a hairy throat and tore it open. His left hand, missing the throat of the other beast, caught and broke its foreleg. A short yelp, the only cry in that grim battle, and hideously human-like, burst from the maimed beast. At the sick horror of that cry from a bestial throat, Conan involuntarily relaxed his grip.

One, blood gushing from its torn jugular, lunged at him in a last spasm of ferocity, and fastened its fangs on his throat—to fall back dead, even as Conan felt the tearing agony of its grip.

The other, springing forward on three legs, was slashing at his belly as a wolf slashes, actually rending the links of his mail. Flinging aside the dying beast, Conan grappled the crippled horror and, with a muscular effort that brought a groan from his blood-flecked lips, he heaved upright, gripping the struggling, tearing fiend in his arms. An instant he reeled off balance, its fetid breath hot on his nostrils; its jaws snapping at his neck; then he hurled it from him, to crash with bone-splintering force down the marble steps.

As he reeled on wide-braced legs, sobbing for breath, the jungle and the moon swimming bloodily to his sight, the thrash of bat-wings was loud in his ears. Stooping, he groped for his sword, and swaying upright, braced his feet drunkenly and heaved the great blade above his head with both hands, shaking the blood from his eyes as he sought the air above him for his foe.

Instead of attack from the air, the pyramid staggered suddenly and awfully beneath his feet. He heard a rumbling crackle and saw the tall column above him wave like a wand. Stung to galvanized life, he bounded far out; his feet hit a step, halfway down, which rocked beneath him, and his next desperate leap carried him clear. But even as his heels hit the earth, with a shattering crash like a breaking mountain the pyramid crumpled, the column came thundering down in bursting fragments. For a blind cataclysmic instant the sky seemed to rain shards of marble. Then a rubble of shattered stone lay whitely under the moon.

* * *

Conan stirred, throwing off the splinters that half covered him. A glancing blow had knocked off his helmet and momentarily stunned him. Across his legs lay a great piece of the column, pinning him down. He was not sure that his legs were unbroken. His black locks were plastered with sweat; blood trickled from the wounds in his throat and hands. He hitched up on one arm, struggling with the debris that prisoned him.

Then something swept down across the stars and struck the sward near him. Twisting about, he saw it—*the winged one!*

With fearful speed it was rushing upon him, and in that instant Conan had only a confused impression of a gigantic man-like shape hurtling along on bowed and stunted legs; of huge hairy arms outstretching misshapen black-nailed paws; of a malformed head, in whose broad face the only features recognizable as such were a pair of blood-red eyes. It was a thing neither man, beast, nor devil, imbued with characteristics subhuman as well as characteristics superhuman.

But Conan had no time for conscious consecutive thought. He threw himself toward his fallen sword, and his clawing fingers missed it by inches. Desperately he grasped the shard which pinned his legs, and the veins swelled in his temples as he strove to thrust it off him. It gave slowly, but he knew that before he could free himself the monster would be upon him, and he knew that those black-taloned hands were death.

The headlong rush of the winged one had not wavered. It towered over the prostrate Cimmerian like a black shadow, arms thrown wide—a glimmer of white flashed between it and its victim.

In one mad instant she was there—a tense white shape, vibrant with love fierce as a she-panther's. The dazed Cimmerian saw between him and the onrushing death, her lithe figure, shimmering like ivory beneath the moon; he saw the blaze of her dark eyes, the thick cluster of her burnished hair; her bosom heaved, her red lips were parted, she cried out sharp and ringing at the ring of steel as she thrust at the winged monster's breast.

'*Bêlit!*' screamed Conan. She flashed a quick glance at him, and in her dark eyes he saw her love flaming, a naked elemental thing of raw fire and molten lava. Then she was gone, and the Cimmerian saw only the winged fiend which had staggered back in unwonted fear, arms lifted as if to fend off attack. And he knew that Bêlit in truth lay on her pyre on the *Tigress's* deck. In his ears rang her passionate cry: 'Were I still in death and you fighting for life I would come back from the abyss——'

With a terrible cry he heaved upward hurling the stone aside. The winged one came on again, and Conan sprang to meet it, his veins on fire with madness. The thews started out like cords on his forearms as he swung his great sword, pivoting on his heel with the force of the sweeping arc. Just above the hips it caught the hurtling shape, and the knotted legs fell one way, the torso another as the blade sheared clear through its hairy body.

Conan stood in the moonlit silence, the dripping sword sagging in his hand, staring down at the remnants of his enemy. The red eyes glared up at him with awful life, then glazed and set; the great hands knotted spasmodically and stiffened. And the oldest race in the world was extinct.

Conan lifted his head, mechanically searching for the beast-things that had been its slaves and executioners. None met his gaze. The bodies he saw littering the moon-splashed grass were of men, not beasts: hawk-faced, dark-skinned men, naked, transfixed by arrows or mangled by sword-strokes. And they were crumbling into dust before his eyes.

Why had not the winged master come to the aid of its slaves when he struggled with them? Had it feared to come within reach of fangs that might turn and rend it? Craft and caution had lurked in that misshapen skull, but had not availed in the end.

Turning on his heel, the Cimmerian strode down the rotting wharfs and stepped aboard the galley. A few strokes of his sword cut her adrift, and he went to the sweep-head. The *Tigress* rocked slowly in the sullen water, sliding out sluggishly toward the middle of the river, until the broad current caught her. Conan leaned on the sweep, his somber gaze fixed on the cloak-wrapped shape that lay in state on the pyre the richness of which was equal to the ransom of an empress.

5

The Funeral Pyre

Now we are done with roaming, evermore;
No more the oars, the windy harp's refrain;
Nor crimson pennon frights the dusky shore;
Blue girdle of the world, receive again
Her whom thou gavest me.

THE SONG OF BÊLIT

Again dawn tinged the ocean. A redder glow lit the river-mouth. Conan of Cimmeria leaned on his great sword upon the white beach, watching the *Tigress* swinging out on her last voyage. There was no light in his eyes that contemplated the glassy swells. Out of the rolling blue wastes all glory and wonder had gone. A fierce revulsion shook him as he gazed at the green surges that deepened into purple hazes of mystery.

Bêlit had been of the sea; she had lent it splendor and allure. Without her it rolled a barren, dreary and desolate waste from pole to pole. She belonged to the sea; to its everlasting mystery he returned her. He could do no more. For himself, its glittering blue splendor was more repellent than the leafy fronds which rustled and whispered behind him of vast mysterious wilds beyond them, and into which he must plunge.

No hand was at the sweep of the *Tigress*, no oars drove her through the green water. But a clean tanging wind bellied her silken sail, and as a wild swan cleaves the sky to her nest, she sped seaward, flames mounting higher and higher from her deck to lick at the mast and envelop the figure that lay lapped in scarlet on the shining pyre.

So passed the Queen of the Black Coast, and leaning on his red-stained sword, Conan stood silently until the red glow had faded far out in the blue hazes and dawn splashed its rose and gold over the ocean.

For more books visit -
www.classypublishing.com